FAKE BLOOD
FAKE BLOOD
FAKE BLOOD
FAKE BLOOD
FAKE BLOOD

FAKE BLOOD

FAKE BLOOD

For the shy kids
and the slayers

I told myself sixth grade was going to be different.

Hey!

Hi,
Hunter!

Not so fast!

Ivy's in the lead!
Ivy's in the lead!

Not for long.
Wait for me.

Come on, AJ!

WAAAK!

CHAPTER 1

But it looks like it's starting out exactly the same.
Ugh.
First!
Great. Now we have to walk.

How was your trip this summer?
Oh, man! It was bonkers! I got my dad to convince my mom to let me jump!
Jump what?

Bungee jump! It was
WIIIILLLLDDD!

You actually jumped?! I don't think I could do something like that.
Well . . . I did. Did you do that hike thing, Ivy?

Yeah! And we made it to the very top of Mount St. Helens. It was so pretty, I thought my eyes were gonna melt.

WELCOME to Historic
St Johns
What'd you do this summer?
Uh . . . Nothing really.
Come on, you had to do something! You didn't have a single adventure?

I did read like **ten books**!

And?

And, ummm . . .
Oh!

READ!
I won these sweet shades from the library.
And?
That's it.

Why do we even bother trying to catch the bus anyway? We never make it.

AJ's in LOOOOOOVE with the bus. Remember?

I AM NOT!

Tulip
PASTRY SHOP
More like in love with a girl who takes the bus.
She's not wrong.
Drop it. Please.
PASTRIES·COOKIES·DONUTS
BREADS·CAKES·PIE
SINCE 1950
APPLE SEASON

Okay, okay.

Slap.

Clasp.

Slide and lean.

High five.
Low five.

Bring it in.

BLOW IT UP!

We good?
Yeah, we're good.

What's with your pants?
Dude, I grew like four inches during the summer.
Well, your pants sure didn't.

I didn't grow at all.

Aw, such a cute little baby.
Knock it off!

I grew too! Only an inch, though.
Maybe an inch and a half.

You didn't grow an inch.

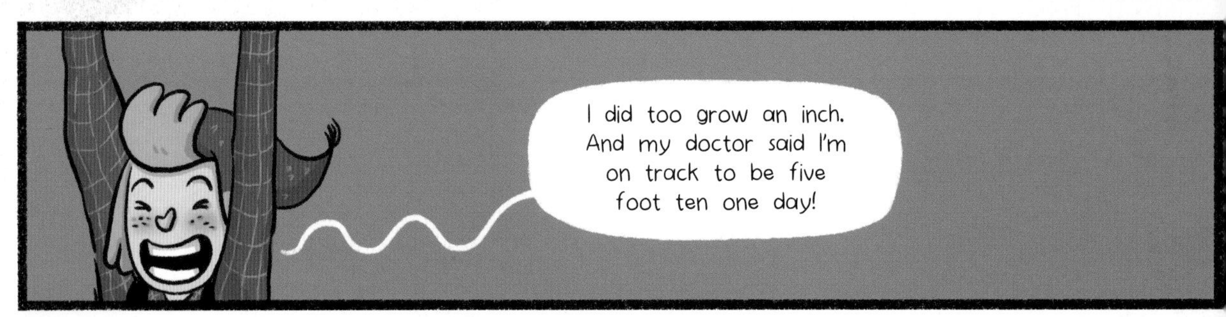
I did too grow an inch. And my doctor said I'm on track to be five foot ten one day!

No way.
Yes way.

SPOONS MIDDLE SCHO
Welcome BACK!
I bet I grow six inches this year alone.
I bet you don't and I do!
You're on.
Why does everything have to be a bet with you two?

Look at all the tiny fifth graders.
Right? I don't remember being that little last year.

I do.

RAAH!
Make way, puny humans! Sixth graders coming through!

MOMENTS LATER
DOUGLAS FIRS
GET YOUR BLOOD
THERE IS NO SUBSTITUTE FOR HARD WORK
WATCH OUT! THE SUN IS FUN BUT HARSH! PROTECT YOURSELF UVA, UVB, UVC CAN BE SCORCHERS
101

And that's why you should never trust a skinny chef.
Get it?
Do you get it?

Right.
Well. I'm Mr. Niles, your new sixth-grade teacher.

Are you from England?

Yeah, are you married to Mary Poppins or something?
Did you take the Tube to school?

Do you drink spotted tea?
I'm from London.
I've never met the woman.
I walked to school.
And I could murder a cup right now.
Now . . .

Say the word tinfoil!

Tinfoil.

Oh. It sounds the same.

You mean **aluminum.**
Aluminum what?

RIGHT.
Let's get on with the roll, shall we?

MR. NILES
WHAM!!
Oh jeez. I'm sorry I'm so late.

Mary Potter
Don't Mess With Witches
MARY POTTERS BOOK 5
The bus totally like went
"KABLAMMO"
this morning.
Like BAM!
BUSTED.
A Woman's Guide to the WILD
THE VAMPIRE —A CASEBOOK—

W- w- whoops!
Dang it!
SURVIVAL IN THE WILD
Moonlight
ADVENTURE JILL
This is why I need more e-books.

Have a seat, and do try to be on time in the future. You never know what you might be missing.
Interesting choice.
THE VAMPIRE
A CASEBOOK
THE VAMPIRE A CASEBOOK
ALAN DUNDES

Wow. Thanks.

There are three things that I know about Nia Winters.

Two, she's absolutely crazy about vampires.
V

And three, even though I really like her and I'd try to catch her bus every day for the rest of my life so we could sit next to each other and maybe one day even hold hands or whatever . . .

ACHOO
Bless you.
WEL OME

MR. NILES
SCHEDU
She has no idea I exist.

MILK
MILK

Oh, man. I missed frosting.

And sprinkles.

I missed cupcakes so much.

Your mom again?
She had us all go off sugar this summer.
SUGAR, MAN. SUGAR.

Do you know how many things have sugar in them?

A lot?

Literally everything. No joke.

Did you guys watch *Fang Squad* last night?

It was actually pretty scary.

No one watches *Fang Squad* but you.

And Nia.

UGH!
Just talk to her already.

Like it's so easy.
You talk to me every day of your life and I'm a girl.
You don't count.
42

Thanks a lot.

Look at her, Ivy.

There's no way she would ever be interested in some boring guy like me.
Not unless you grow some gnarly fangs.

Yeah, right.

How's the new teacher? Mr. . . .

Niles. He's okay. Seems pretty strict.
That sucks.

Vacuums suck, BB.

Fine. Stinks.
That stinks.

He's British or something.
He's got an accent.

Now that's
hot.

HACK!

He's a little old for you, B.
Anyway.

So, AJ, how are all your friends doing this year? How's Hunter, Ivy . . .
Nia?

The same. Everyone's the same.
Well, that's good, right?

I just thought, I don't know, sixth grade would be more . . .

Ma-ture?

CLANG!
I guess.
I just feel . . .

exactly the same as ever.

Thanks for dinner, Mom.
I'm going to my room.
Oh. All right.

You sure you're okay, AJ?
Need anything? You don't
want ice cream or—
No!
I'm fine!

ALIENS
Lucinda!
You don't understand!

If I bite you, you'll be forced to join the Fang Squad.
You won't have a choice!
Oh, Marius.
SNAP!
What if I don't want a choice?!

GROSS

Is that *Fang Squad*?!
No!

You know,
I don't feel any different either.
And I'm way older than you.
You're fifteen.

Exactly.

You're a girl.

So?

So, it's different for girls.
Girls are already mysterious
and cool.

POOT!
How's that for mysterious and cool?

You're disgusting.

Yeah, and I'm a girl. I'm no different than a dude.

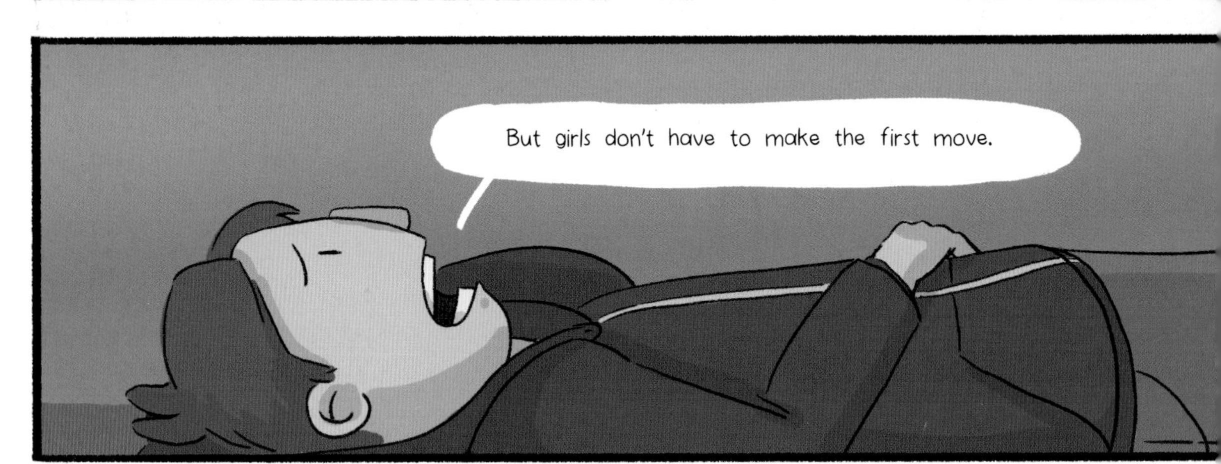
But girls don't have to make the first move.

Okay, that's such a lie. You don't even know.
Why the heck not?
Well, she's never gonna talk to me first.
Because I'm me. I'm boring.

All eleven-year-olds are boring.
So she's boring too.

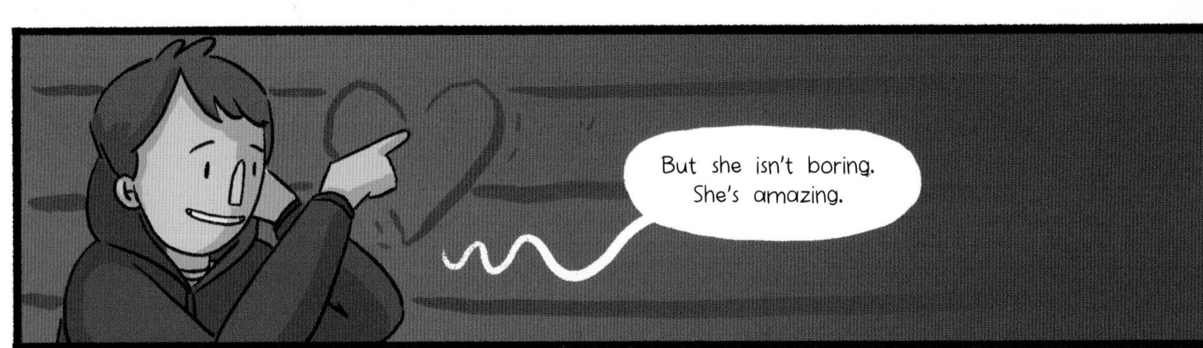
But she isn't boring. She's amazing.

No one is so amazing that you can't just talk to them.
BB, what would I even say? What am I gonna do?

Just be yourself. I always am, and I'm wonderful.
You dork.
You love it.

Maybe?

SIGH

CHAPTER 2

TOTALLY AMAZING SCIENCE -FACTS-

What if we just kick around my hacky sack?

I can't let Ivy win this bet!

Hacky sack won't make you taller. Can I please just finish my book?

But it's recess! We should be having fun.

Exactly.

FIIIIINE!

Enough's enough.

Hunter! Give it back.

Look, just go over there and say hi to Nia. That's all you have to do.
It's NOT that easy! Stop acting like it is!

Go, dude! She's looking at you.

No!
THE HUNTED

Are they fighting?
Eh, yes and no.

Here, dude. I'm sorry, okay?
S'all right.
TOTALLY AWESOME
SCIENCE FACTS!

Does AJ look
a little . . .
Strange?
You mean shorter?
Nah.
It just looks like
it because of how
tall I am now.

All right!
Line up!
C'mon, man.
Let's go.

I have some exciting news!
Today we begin our first project. I'll be splitting the class into pairs.
That's fun, right?
PUMPING
WORK
SCORCHERS
Each pair will select a location, anywhere in the world. . . .

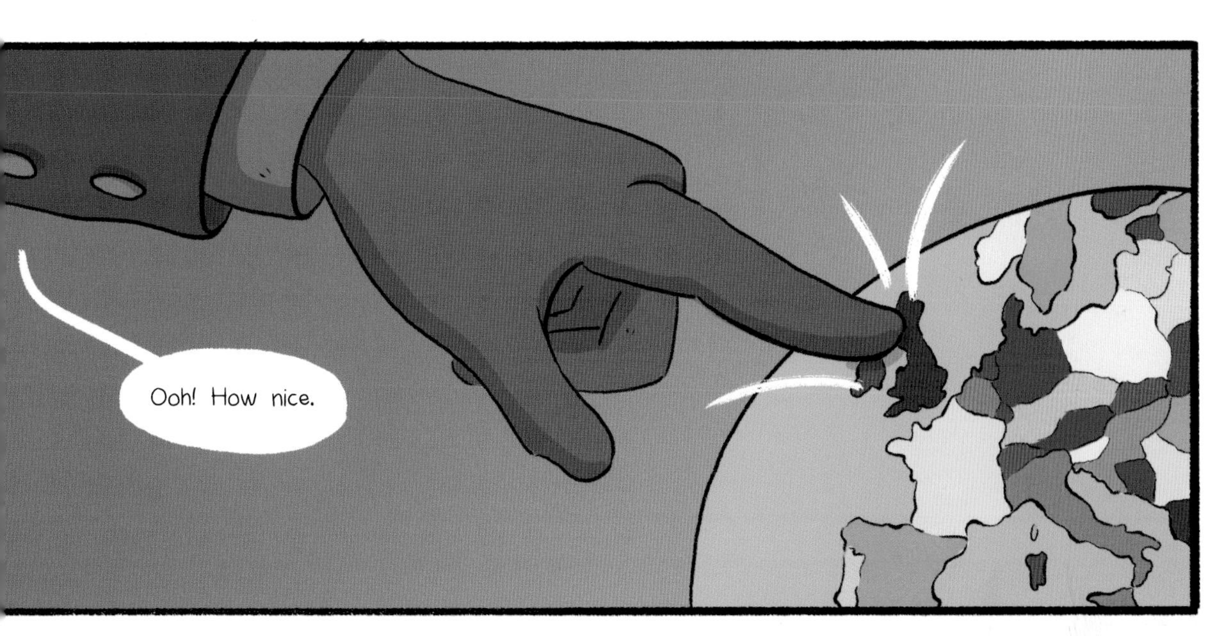
Ooh! How nice.

And will create a report to present to the class.

Let's choose Tasmania or something fun like that!
Yeah, cool!

I'm terribly sorry to disappoint, Mr. Hunter, but I will be choosing your partners.
You are with Miss Ivy.

Huh?! Present!
I'm here!

We're doing what now?
You're my partner for the project, shorty.

Snap to, young lady. We don't want to be left behind already, do we?
No, Mr. Niles.

Good. Lovely shirt by the way. It's the same color as my house!
Um . . . okay.

Now, Mr. Brooks is with Mr. Brent. Miss Liz and Mr. Roger. And Mr. AJ, you're with Miss Nia.
Pair up, and pick a geographical location!

So!
What about a place with a really funky name?
Uh-huh.
She's talking to me.

Like Kyrgyzstan or Djibouti. Ha!
Booty. Weird.
WORLD ATLAS
WORLD ATLAS

She just said booty, oh my God.
Sure.

You okay?

You look real pale.
You match Antarctica.
Antarctica

Yeah. I'm fine. Whatever you want.
Just keep looking at me.

Ohhhhkay.

I know what we should do! It's perfect.
Where?

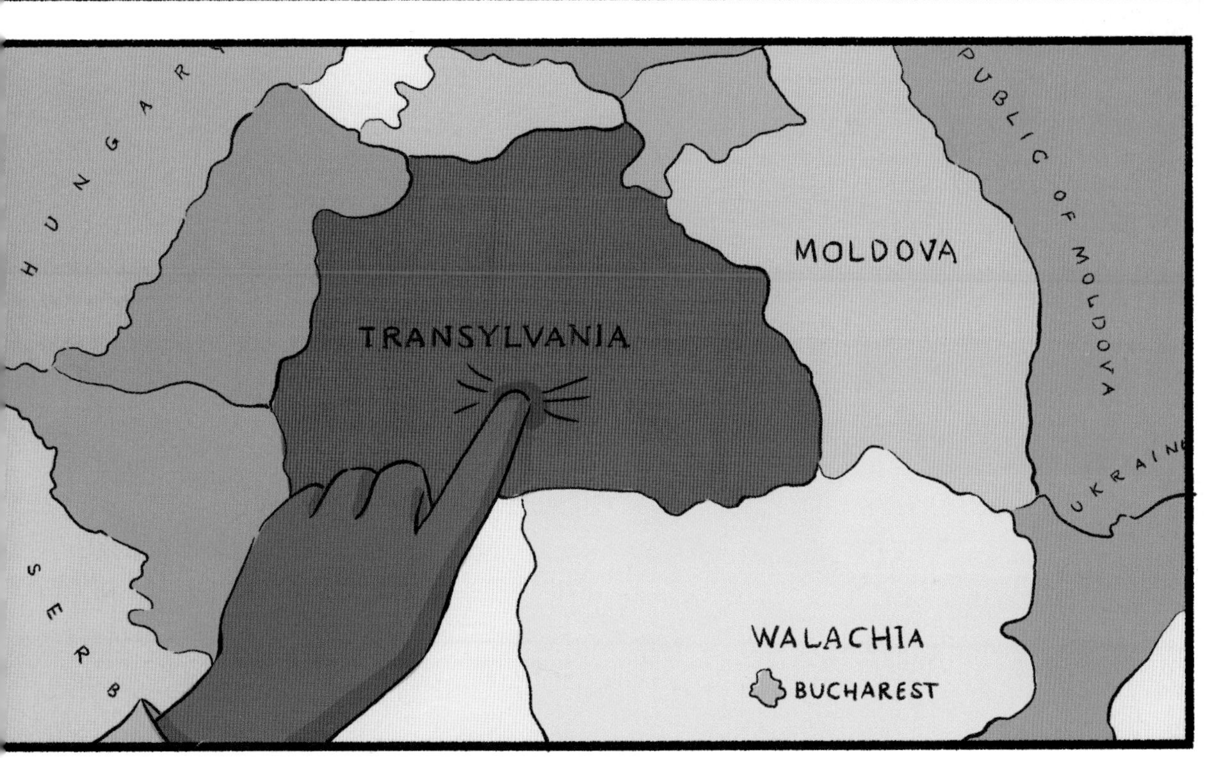
MOLDOVA
TRANSYLVANIA
WALACHIA
BUCHAREST

Now, I've been seeing a lot of the same comments lately.

Everyone wants to know how I get my bun so big!

The secret is simple, and a Portland staple. Doughnuts.

Moonlight
MOONLIGHT
BETHANY FRYER

You won't drain me. You're not like the rest of them!
How do you know?

I can feel it . . . in my bones.

You don't know anything about me!
I know you're a vampire!

Don't! You'll—

They're not even in Transylvania!

Ha!
Beat that.

Easy.

YES!
No!

You cheated!

How could she cheat at throwing a rock?

You throw one, AJ. Do that skipping thing.
Oh yeah! Last time it went like fifty feet!
It's really cool.

It's not cool. It's dumb.

No, it's not!
Come on!
Do it! Do it!

Vile!
That was incredible!
It skipped like a million times!
Do you think you could teach me?
Me too!
Maybe tomorrow. I should get going.
MOONLIGHT
MOONLIGHT O ORPHAN

Thanks for cheering me up, you guys.

So Transylvania's population is . . .
PROPERTY OF SPOONS M.S.

WWW.TRANSYLVANIAFACTS.INFO
TRANSYLVANIA
POPULATION:
6,608,586

Do you think that includes immortal undead bloodsuckers?
Is that a joke?

Yes? No. I- I- I don't know.

I never joke about vampires.

Stop trying to be cool. You're not cool.
Sorry. I'm not like trying to be mean or anything.
No, of course not.

I just take that stuff super serious. You know?
Totally.
WORLD HISTORY
WORLD HISTORY

TICK TACK
TICK TACK
TICK TACK
TICK TACK

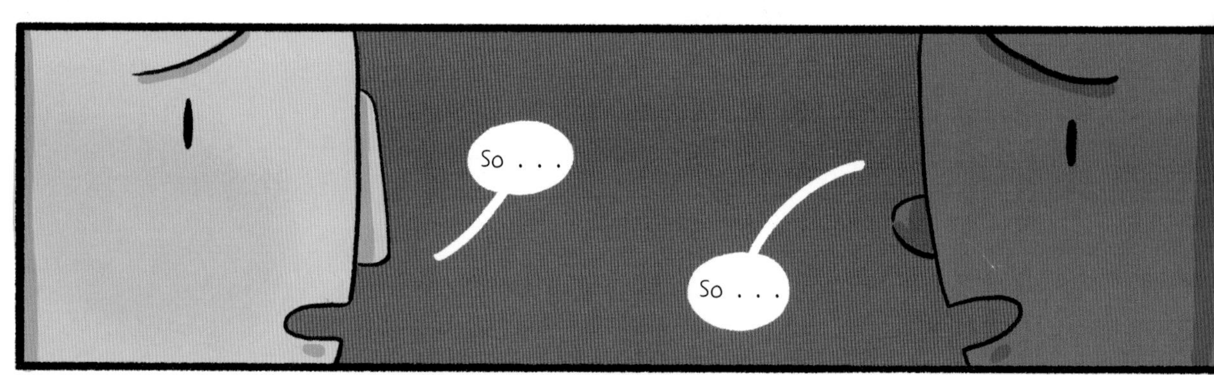
So . . .
So . . .

Whoa.
Did you know there's a real Dracula's Castle?

Oh yeah! It's called Bran Castle, right?

Yes! Of course you'd know. You're really smart.

Oh my gosh, Nia. It's for sale.
WHAT?!

There's a lot of chitchatting coming from this table.

Sorry, Mr. N. But we just found out some **epic news** about our—

Maybe you two should stick to books for now, if the Internet is going to cause such a distraction.
I assure you a good old-fashioned paper book has just as much to offer as any gadget.
PROPERTY OF SPOONS M.S.
So let's trade, shall we?

Right, right,
good, good.
Um. This is
a dictionary.
We have
plenty of books.

The castle thing
is still really cool.

It's official.
I'm obsessed
with vampires.

CLICK!

SMOKEY
NIGHTS

'Sup?

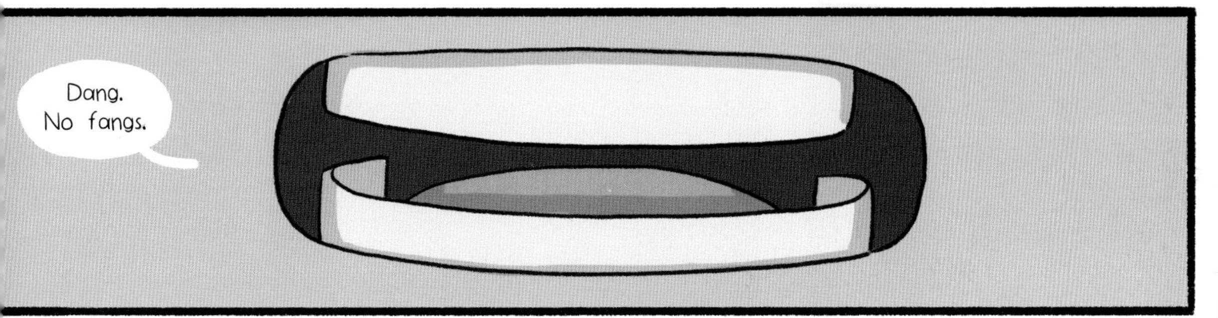
Dang.
No fangs.

TK
TK
TK
TK
TK

IVY
Ivy. I need your help.
Yeah?
Tell me everything you know about vampires.
Trade you for those platforms BB wears.
Deal.

Get away from me with that!

CHAPTER
3

Glitter is the best I could come up with!
How else are you going to look prismatic?
I don't want to look prismatic!

But that's what happens to vampires in the sun! I thought you wanted to be accurate!
Not that accurate.

SIGH

Oh, well.

I guess it doesn't matter. I still got your sister's shoes.

And it's cloudy out today.

Hey, guys!

What's on your face? You look like a raccoon.

Nothing! I'm just tired.

Why are you covered in sparkles? Is it Halloween?

It's a vampire thing.

Vampires don't sparkle.
That's what I said!

It's the best I could do.
I don't know how to
radiate rainbows, okay?

That's the silliest thing
I've ever heard.

Seriously!
I thought vampires
burst into flames
in a big blood-and-
guts explosion!

WAGH BLEH

What Nia plan?
Fine.
I guess you don't really care about this whole Nia plan.

Ivy. **Please.** Don't.

Hey, Hunter . . .

You want my snack cakes?

HECK YES!

Go get 'em!

You didn't even get the outfit right.

Did you even look up photos online?

You don't have the belt.

Your hair is all flat and wrong.

Where are your sunglasses?

I didn't think I'd need them.

Dude. Vampires go into shade when they're in the sun. They can't help it.

What?
It's not a fashion choice. They just appear.

You really should finish the book.

I'm never finishing *Moonlight*. Never.

Got the cakes!
You sure did.

SPOONS MIDDLE SCHOOL
Come on, AJ. Put in a little effort. Don't you think she's worth it?

Now **this** is the breakfast of champions!

Ivy.
What even is that supposed to be?

It's for our project.
It's that arch thing.
In France.
Obviously.

L'ARC
DE
TRIOMPHE!

Yeah.
That.

You need to add all the angels and horses and stuff.
Can I show you?

Fine.

Ch-ch-check it out!
It's Bran Castle.

It's so good!
I like the for sale sign.

That was my own personal addition.

FOR SALE

It's perfect.

Dorks.

Are you sure you're feeling okay lately?
I think so?

You look like majorly sleepy. Like walking dead status.

Oh . . . um . . . Hey, you should put a vampire in the window.
Yeah! Looking out all spooky-like.

What I wouldn't give to come face-to-face with a real vampire.

You **really** like vampires, huh?

Like isn't the right word.

GULP!

And zen you add zee leetle tails on zee horses!

And because zis iz France zee horses wear leetle berets!

Do more!

But of course!

All zee angels get striped shirts and ah! Zey are so sad because zey are Franch!
Also a croissant.

Magnifique!
Oui, oui!

And *voila*!
It's my masterpiece!
You're so funny, Hunter!
It looks awesome!

Those are
my supplies!

Ugh.

Sorry.

I'm so sorry.

That was weird. I'll get your stuff. Sorry. Sorry.

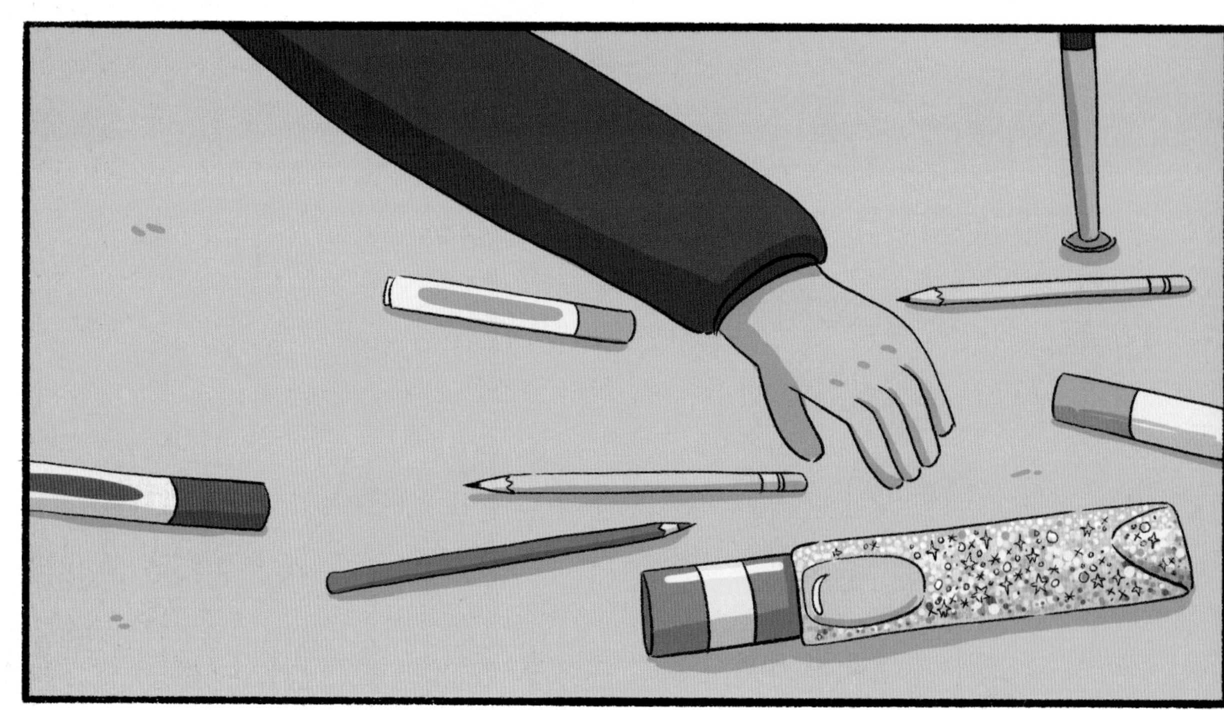

Here, Ivy.
Really. I didn't
mean—

Dude, it's okay.
Yeah, we all get
weird sometimes.

Maybe you just need
to get more sun.
Heh.

AJ, you can do this.

She's worth the effort.

If I suck your blood, you'll be stuck in the Fang Squad . . .

For liiiiife.

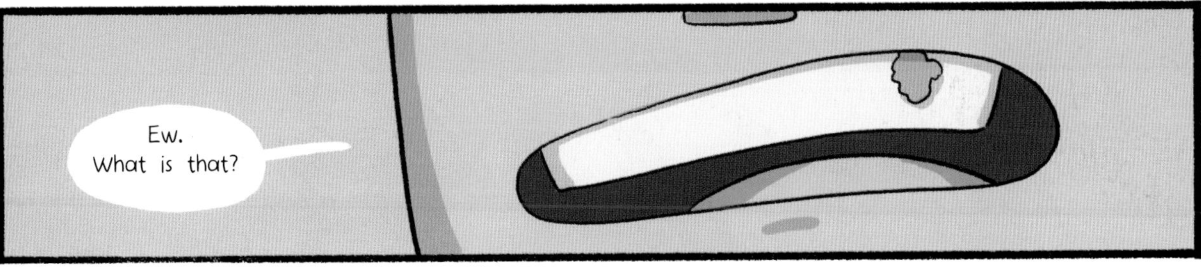
Ew.
What is that?

Where can I get some . . .
Oh! I know!

NO.
NO.
NOPE.
Bingo!

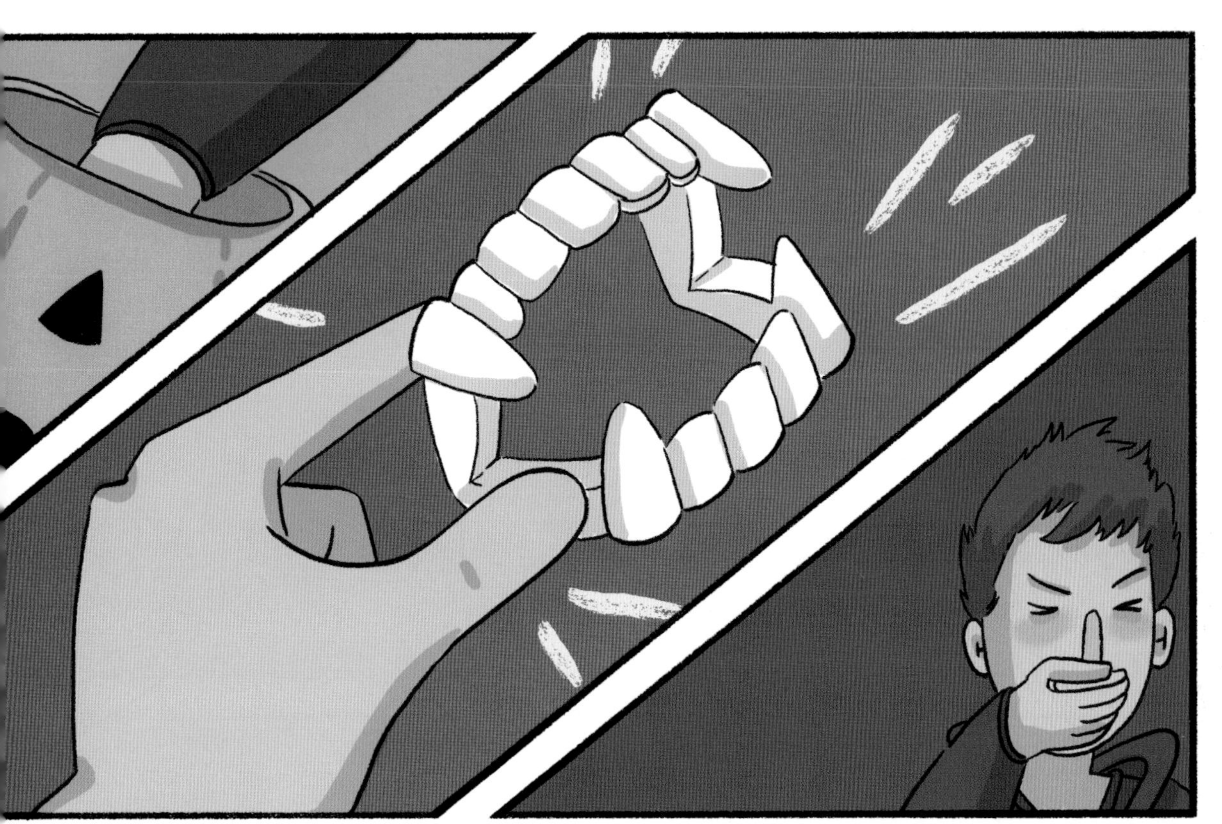

You'll be in the Fang Squad FOR LIFE!

Dude,
you went all out.
It's a big improvement.

THANKSS

Oh no.
Those have
to go.

Thith ith
the betht I got!

What?
I thaid, thit- OW!

Blech. The plastic cut me.

The drool? Not cute.

Do you sleep anymore, man? You look drained.
I'm fine.

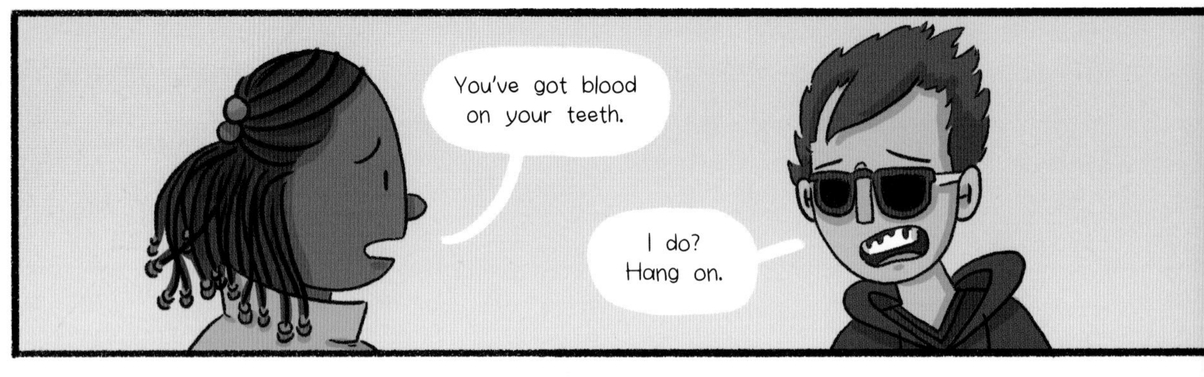
You've got blood on your teeth.
I do? Hang on.

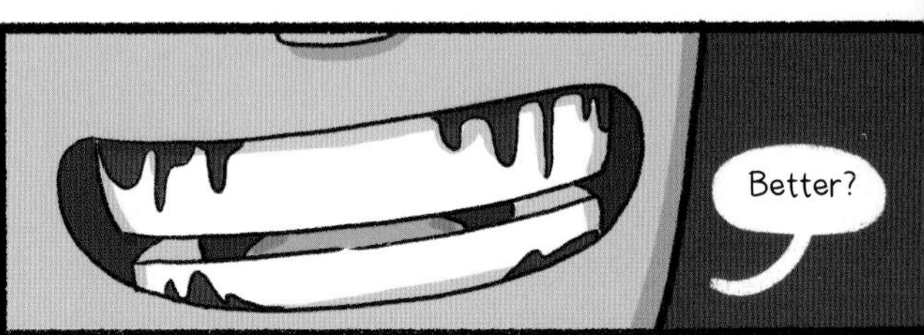
Better?

Worse.
Much worse.

What was in that bottle?

It's nothing! I mean, it's water. Just water. I um . . .

I'll be right back!

BACK 2 SCHOOL PARTY! FRIDAY @ 5PM
SOCIETY
EVERY TUES
ART CLUB WEDNESDAY

ROBOTICS CLUB TUESDAY
NEW
BACK 2 SCHOOL PARTY! FRIDAY @ 5PM
ART CLUB WEDNESDAY

I look crazy . . .
I look scary . . .
I look . . .

REAL

Do you need the nurse?
No, I vant to suck your blood!

Sick, dude!
You do look pretty vampy, though.
Wait, wait. Just look.
I'm sorry, Nia, you're just a girl,
and I'm immortal.

Any taller?
TUESDAY
FRIDAY
THURSDAY

Not yet.

Crud.

Hey, if you're a vampire, I'm that wolf guy!

Wait, what?

AWOOOOOO

Hunter, no.

Pre-teen wolf! Rahrr!

I'm TRANSFORMING!

What's going on in here?!

Nothing!
We're leaving!

I thought I heard . . . yelling?
Nope.
Not at all!
Howling?
Ha, ha!
Of course not.

BRRING
Phones ain't allowed, teach.
At least put it on vibrate.

I know, blast it!
I know.
I can never get it to . . .

Let me help you.
No! I've got it.
I can do it!

There. Fixed. Done.
Okay?

Now. Get on your way.
Chop, chop!
Aye-aye, sir.

We really had him spooked, huh?
Spooked?

Yeah! The monster bros!
The gruesome twosome.

Up high!

You know, this is sort of my . . .

AWOOOOOO

Maybe I was wrong.

BUS STOP

Maybe this year **will** be different.

CHAPTER 4

AJ?
AJ? That's you, right?

Oh, hey, Nia.

You're taking the bus now?
I uh, just uh . . . you know, thought I'd try it out.

It's a real thrill, huh?

Yeah. Cool. Whatever.

Okay. Well, I'm almost done with my book, so . . .

What are you reading?!

Uhh . . . Where's the book?

Audiobook.

Sounds fun.
It is!
It's this book about this girl ninja. She's like this super assassin. And no one knows! Not even her parents.

You've probably never heard of—
You're reading *Natalie and the Ninja Star*?!
YES!

This is your stop, kids.

Oh.
Right.

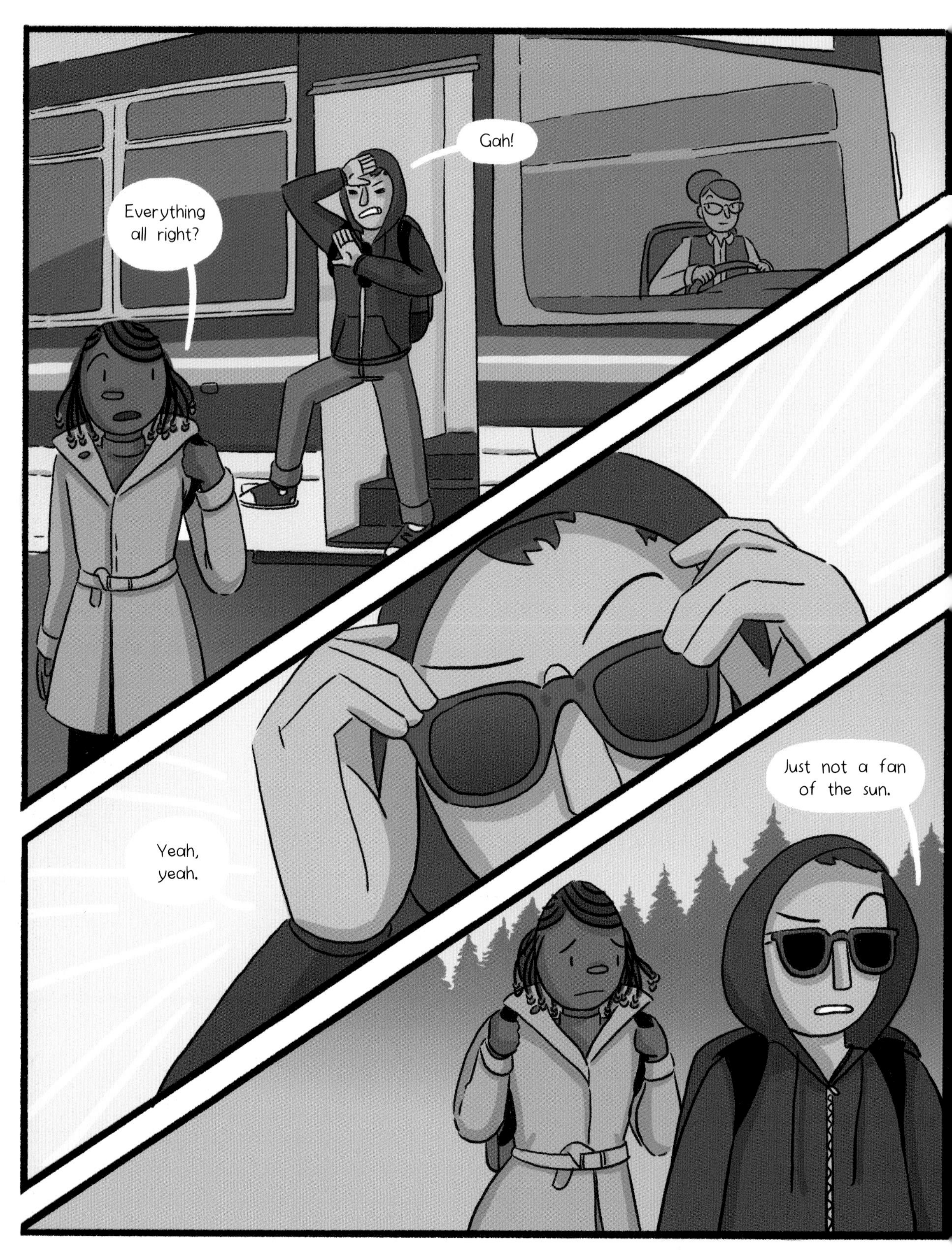
Everything all right?
Gah!
Yeah, yeah.
Just not a fan of the sun.

READING
IS THE KEY.
In sanguine salubritas.
I . . .
You . . .
Well . . .

One moment.

Now, what was I saying?

The project.
Right, well. You'll present your reports next week. Don't be lazy.
Endeavour to include rich details. Expound upon the climate, the cuisine, the culture.

You're doing well.
I find that I'm
discovering new things
along with you.

Like what?!

Oh, just
little
trivialities.

Facts about cacti,
crepes . . .

and
castles.

BRIIING!
Yes! Lunch!

Cheers, mate.

Uh . . .
Cheers.

RAH!
GRAHH H!

Your costume is looking good, man.

It's not a costume.

When I found these in my attic, I was like, perfect!
It's real wolf fur.

Really?

Absolutely. Where are your fangs?

I don't need them.
I just use this.
GENUINE
FAKE BLOOD

Only a vampire can crush on you . . . forever.
Good one, dude.
UGH! I can't believe I'm still so puny.
You're taller than I am.

You think that's helping?
It's worth a shot. What else am I gonna do?

You guys didn't even bet anything. Who cares if you lose?

I do!
I care!
And so does Ivy.
You're almost there!

But I'm not
just a ninja.
I'm Natalie.

RAHHH!
WAHHH!

Where's my stuff, nerd-o?
What stuff?
Don't play dumb. I know you took them.
Took what?

Let's see.
My blue shoes?
My eye shadow?

It's all missing. Where is it?

W-why would I want your shoes?

Maybe you gave them to that girl?
Ivy wouldn't ever want—
Not her.
Not Ivy. That other girl, the one you like! You can't just give her my stuff. That's no way to get a girl to like you!
I didn't give her anything!
Really?
Yes!

MOONLIGHT
MOONLIGHT FRYER
And what are you doing with this?!

I wanted to read it!

You made fun of me when I bought it!

You're being so weird with your sneaking and your new hair!
Hey! I'm sorry!

I'm watching you.

Fine!

And my stuff.

OKAY I GET IT!

Thief.

Snoop.

G'nite.
Night.

Hey. You're back!
Hey.

Couldn't get enough of that bus lifestyle, huh?

Mmm hmm.

Yeah. Right.

Oh snap!
My search alert!
BWEEP
BWEEP

What's that for?

I created a search alert, so anytime something new is posted about Bran Castle, an alarm sounds.

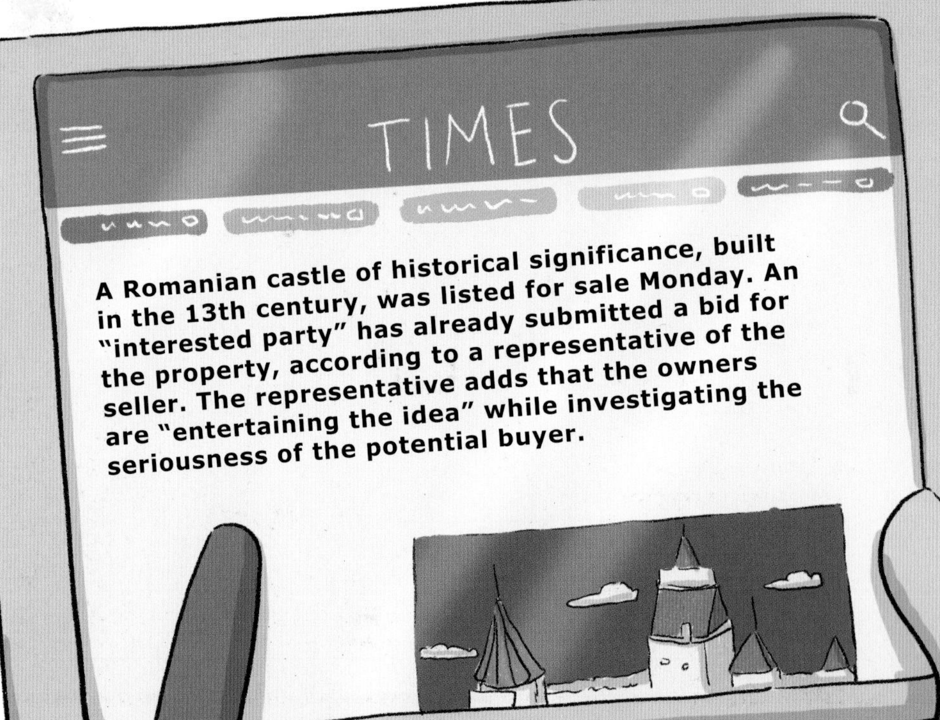
TIMES

A Romanian castle of historical significance, built in the 13th century, was listed for sale Monday. An "interested party" has already submitted a bid for the property, according to a representative of the seller. The representative adds that the owners are "entertaining the idea" while investigating the seriousness of the potential buyer.

Why write an article at all, if you aren't gonna say anything in it?
Bummer.
So.
Umm . . .
Umm . . .
So . . .
Is the audiobook different from the paper book?
No, but it's fun because the girl who reads it is like really animated and she gets super into it.

Wanna listen with me?

Have a good day, kids.

Bye!
Thanks for the ride!

What's that you have there?
It's my mom's old tablet. I use it for games and books and stuff.

Your mother knows how to use that thing?
Yeah, it's easy.
Gracious, I'm old.

Can you get Hemo to work?

I don't think I have that app. What's it called?

Oh, forget it.

I can help you. I help my mom with her phone all the time.
It's nothing. Never mind. Just silly phone stuff. Stupid, you know.

BRRING!
Now, in you go.
Time for class.

Psst.
Want to listen
to the book
. . .

at recess?

YES!

Recess recess recess recess recess recess recess recess recess recess . . .

Recess recess recess
recess recess recess
recess recess
RECESS RECESS
Green!
Purple!

Recess recess
recess recess
recess

You will never . . .
recess
recess
recess

EVER . . .
be five foot ten!
YES . . .
I . . .
WILL!

I swear if you don't stop—
Uh . . .
Stop what, Ivy? Stop growing?

TWEEP!
That's enough! Get to the office. Now!

MAIN OFFICE
BE YOUR OWN HERO

CHAPTER 5

Can we at least—

Not another word.

BRRING
Hush, now!
I can't believe you guys.
I'm so glad you called.

You ruined everything.

I didn't leave that many messages.

Why's he so upset?
I dunno.

It doesn't matter. Listen, everything's going to be different now.

Who cares who's taller? It's so dumb.

Chill, dude.
Come on, don't be mad.

Because, darling, I got you a gift.
Something incredible.

Why shouldn't I be mad?
All you two ever do is fight.

Oh, please. It's not really fighting.
We're just having fun! You know that.

Of course it matters.
You don't know what it is yet!

It isn't fun! It's stupid!

CHILDREN!

Darling? Hello?

Good-bye, I guess.

SIGH

ULTIMATE VAMPIRE

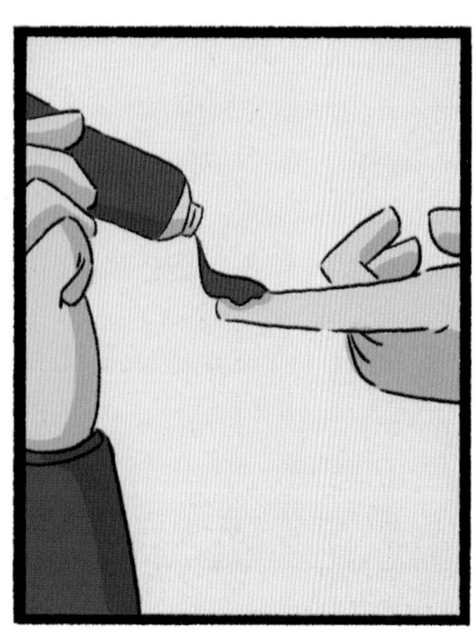

Mr. Niles? I'm, I'm . . .

BLEEDING.

W-what?

We should take him to the nurse!
Yeah, or to the—

No!

Mr. AJ . . .
Come here.

You couldn't have waited?
Is it bad?

Go. Go now, to the nurse or wheresoever you see fit. Just begone.

Should I—

Just go. Now. Before anyone sees you.

I'm going. I'm going.

BADMINTON SOCIETY
EVERY TUESDAY
BACK 2
Hey, AJ! Wait up!

That was quite the pile up y'all had in the cafeteria, huh?
Sorry you got in trouble.

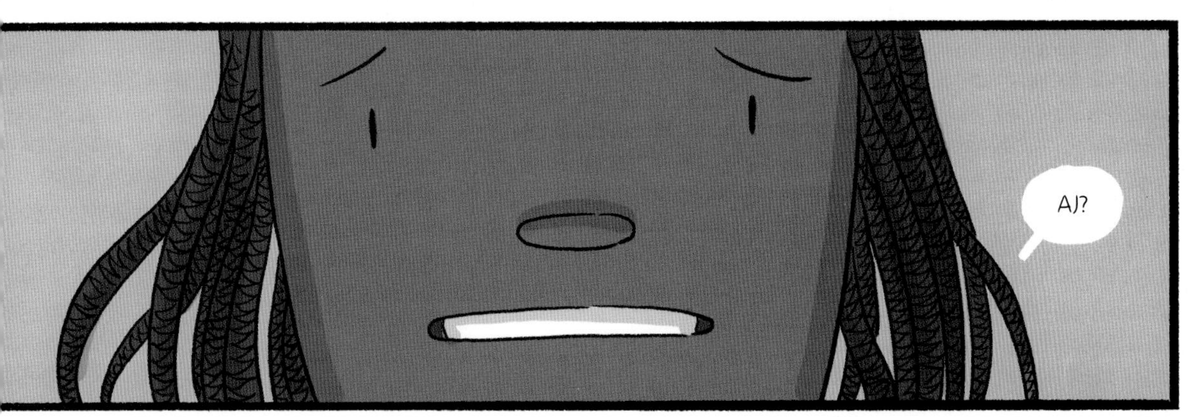
AJ?

Yeah?
Ummm . . . There's blood in your mouth . . . again.

I wouldn't worry about it.
Why not?
It's, like, personal.
You're acting really weird.

It's all good.
Okay . . . Well, do you want to work on our project later?

YES!
I mean, yeah sure. Sounds cool.

I guess I'll see you on the bus then?
If you're not too hurt or busy or whatever.

We can listen to the book on the way. If you want.
Totally.

It's working!

Everything all right, Mr. AJ?
I don't know how you stomach that stuff.

I know it's all the rage now but I just . . .
I have no taste for it at all.

Taste for what?
The fake stuff.

You knew it was fake?

Of course! Why wouldn't it be? No one has the real stuff anymore.
It's all synthetic this and soylent that these days.

Mr. Niles, what are you talking about?
Um . . . What are *you* talking about?

Because it sounds like . . .

BRRING!
BACK 2 SCHOOL PAR
Hey! There goes that pesky bell. Back to class! Mustn't be late!
ART CLUB

We're gonna race home!
You can time us!

Come on!
You're not still mad,
are you?
No.

I'm not mad, I'm just done.

Done with what?

Trying to compete with you guys!

You weren't even in on the bet.

Yeah! I know! You always leave me out of them. Because I'm too boring or dorky or whatever.

We never said—

You didn't have to! You both think you're so great, bungee jumping and mountain climbing and all that.

Not cool!

Neither of you is any better than the other. Neither of you is better than me.

Dude, harsh.

Whatever.

Listen, just because—
Let him go, Ivy. Obviously, he's better off without us.

BUS STOP

Hey.
Hi.

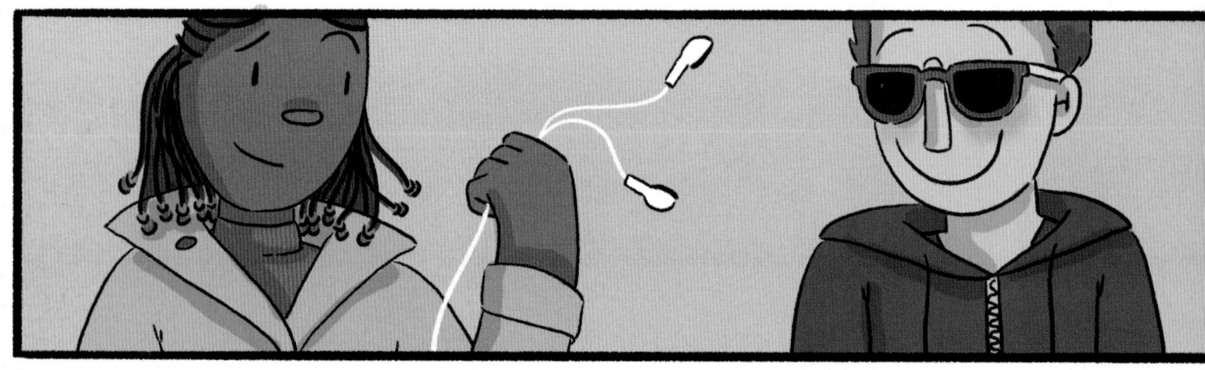

You know, I can't thank you enough for all your hard work!
And thank you for saving the library. I couldn't have done it without you.

Who knew that the answers were in the encyclopedia the whole time?!

You know what I always say . . .

If you don't know where to look, the answer's probably in a book.

I like that book a lot.
They're making a second one.
What? I had no idea!

Yeah! I'm super excited. Powell's is going to throw a party when it comes out.
We should go together!

Oh, um.

Did I just ask her out?!?!

Oh, gosh. I mean. Um. I was just trying to say that it would be, you know . . .

No. I get it. It's just . . .

What?

READ!
I know.
You do?

I've been paying attention.

Well, you're just . . . The coolest girl I've—
What?
What, what?

It's not fair.
I'm so confused.

I've been waiting for like forever to meet someone like you and now, like when I do, it's like I'm worried I'm gonna lose my nerve.

How come?
Because I'm not supposed to like vampires.
Wait. You're not?

I'm supposed to . . .
SLAY THEM.

HOLY H2O

Wait, wait! You've got it all wrong.

You can't trick me now. I've figured it out.

This is just a big mix-up!

A mix-up? I highly doubt that. I have mountains of proof!

First, you had that big fight with Hunter.

Because he pushed you into the sunlight at recess!

Are you kidding? I love the sun!
It's totally like my favorite thing!
So bright! So yellow!

And your eyes.

They're all sunken in!
I'm an insomniac!
Oh, please!

You started taking the bus so you didn't have to walk in the sun.

And your sunglasses!
Who wears sunglasses in the fall?
In Portland?

READ!
I got these at the library! I read a lot! You know that!
And your teeth? Bloody!

It's not real!

Why would you fake something like that?

Please, you have to believe—

It'll be over quick. I promise.

You don't have to do this.

If it makes you feel any better, I thought you were pretty great.

You know, before the whole bloodsucker thing.

Really?

You can't run forever!

Pant
Pant
Pant
Pant

What is . . .

HAPPENING?!

HIC

You all right in there? I heard the door slam.

I'm fine!
Just had the worst day ever, of my life, that's all.

Are you sure? Because it's okay if you need to—
Yes, Mom. Dang!

Just checking, Mr. Attitude.

SIGH

CHAPTER 6

Come on, Ivy! I said I was sorry.

I need your help!!

Hey, Hunter.
Hey, Ivy.
HELLO?

Guys! It's an EMERGENCY!

Did you bring them?
Yeah, see? We're gonna look so Franch!

I'M TALKING LIFE AND DEATH HERE!

It looks good on you!
We're totally gonna ace this thing.

WATCH OUT! THE SUN IS FUN BUT HARSH!
PROTECT YOURSELF
UVA, UVB, UVC CAN BE
SCORCHERS
Can we have until Friday?

All right, today's the last day to work on your projects in class.
We still have a whole section to finish!

I'm failing to see how that is my problem.

No, it's just—

It's a really big project and—

I'm hearing a lot of . . . excuses.
I do not like excuses.

So get to work.

Truce.
For now.
Oh, sure.
Okay.

Good.

I can't just behead you here, ya know?

How about you don't behead me at all?!

I already told you, I feel bad about it, but it is what it is.

Mr. Niles is acting weird today, don't you think?
Maybe he's burning out.

Or he's just having a bad day.

It feels like there's something . . .

What's that?
My half of the report.

Wow, AJ. It looks really good. Like super profesh.
It's just a binder.
Don't be so modest. The crest was a great idea.

TRANSYLVANIA
A REPORT BY NIA AND AJ

I like the maps and the charts and stuff.
TRANSYLVANIA
I traced them out of some books.
Do you think I could color them in?
Of course! That would look much prettier.

Stop it, okay?
Sorry. I'll shut up.

It's just, you're making it hard for me to want to . . . you know . . .

STAB! STAB!

Exactly.

Well, you don't have to.
Yeah, actually, I do.

IT'S LIKE MY DESTINY!

Oh.

I guess I could give you a head start.

A head start? What do you mean?

Let's see.
I won't start
hunting you . . .

Hunting me?!
No!

until five
minutes

after the last bell.

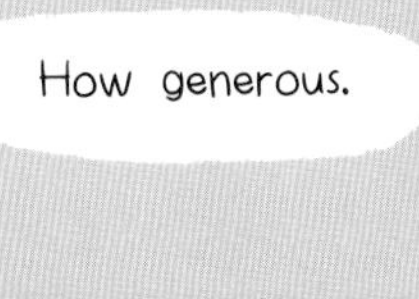
How generous.

You're
welcome.

You're going down.
In your dreams.

What's the bet?

I've been preparing for this moment all year.
That's cute. I don't need to prepare.

Do you need me to time you guys?
Keep score?

Ready?
Set?
GO!
Guys, please.

I was just jealous.

Both of you get to do all this exciting stuff, and all I ever do is like . . .

SNRF

CRONCH!

read.

And I know it's boring to you,
but I actually like reading.

Are you guys listening?

Yoink!

MUNCH!!

I win!
You cheater!

HELLOOOOO?!

Rematch?

I never really thought about how I would die.

Mr. Niles?
Where's Hunter?
Ah, um, he had to go home. He was feeling rather poorly.

Yes! I SO win.

But dying at the hands of someone you love might not be the worst way to go.
SPOONS MIDDLE SCHO
FIVE MINUTES!

SIGNAL
SIGNAL
PIZZA

FALL
SALE
I see you!
SLASHING PRICES!
ONE DAY LEFT
EVERYTHING MUST GO!

PORTLAND

Hey!

It's not fair!
I just wanted to be cool.
Interesting.
Grown up.

And now my best friends won't talk to me and the love of my life wants to cut my head off.

Darling? It's me again.

I have some news!

Everything is ready.
I'm packing the last of my—

What do you mean you aren't coming?
What's he got that—

Is this some sort of cruel joke?

Darling?
Hello?
What happened?

Stupid contraption!
Forget it all!

Why do I bother?

Hmm.
I think he broke it.

Gotcha!

AHH
NOOO

I swear I'm not a vampire. You have to—you have to believe me. I was just pretending. So that you'd . . . like me.
I know.

You know?!

Your bag broke.

GENUINE FAKE BLOOD
And this fell out.

So, you know, sorry?

Nia!

You were gonna murder me!
Only for like a day. I said I was sorry.

So you're disappointed you don't get to actually kill me?

Yes and no?

Harsh.

Hey, this was like my dream, okay?
I didn't want to kill you.
But did I want to be a slayer?

Uh.
Duh.

Now that dream is over.

What if I told you it might not be?

So . . . have you noticed how Mr. Niles has been really tired lately?
Maybe it's Seasonal Affective Disorder from all the clouds. He did just move here.

Could be. But what if it's something else?

What do you mean?

What if Mr. Niles . . .

No way. He couldn't be a vampire.

Why not?
Because he's gonna be my mentor one day.

Every slayer has a mentor. Usually they're British. He hasn't approached me because he doesn't know I'm a slayer yet.

But what about—

AJ, I know vampires. Trust me.

I do trust you. But really think about it.

I saw his eyes outside, and they were red.

He kept asking for help with his phone.

So I tried to look up the app he wanted help with, and it doesn't exist!

But what does that have to do with vampires?

Ugh. I don't know. I can't figure it out. But you're so . . . You know everything about this stuff and I just thought that—
Okay, okay. Turn it on. Let's check it out.

He threw it in the water. It's broken. A dead end.

RICE! We need some rice! STAT!

Okay, okay, okay. Please don't let go!
You've got this.

Why do you need-

There.

Heeeey, Nia? Your mom is waiting outside.

Oh!
I'll be right there!

Is that gonna fix it?

It just might.
I'm gonna bring it home with me. Is that okay?
Yeah, sure.
No problem.
HONK! HONK!
Hey. I'm glad I didn't have to decapitate you.
You have a nice head.

Yeah, um, okay, see you around. I mean, see you at school. That's where I usually see you.
Later!
AJ and Nia choppin' down a tree!
Hey!
With B-I-G-F-O-O-T!
No!

First comes the drizzle.
Don't!
Then comes the rain.
STOP!
Next thing you know we're popping champagne!

SLAM!
Because it's your wedding.
Because I'm making a toast at your wedding so we're drinking champagne.
Because you're in love with Nia.
Because-
I GET IT!

ALIENS

TNK

TNK
TNK

TNK
TNK
Ivy?

What?
What are you doing here?

You can whisper.

Um, what?

I can't understand you, Ivy.

JUST SAY IT!

Fine.
I guess I lose
the bet.
What bet?

The "who can
go the longest
without talking
to you" bet.

Wow.
Thanks
a lot.

You deserved it.
Okay, yeah.
You're right.

Hey, Ivy?
What are you doing here?
Oh yeah!
HUNTER IS MISSING!

I sent him a text— no response. I called him— no answer. He always answers! He answered when he had chicken pox.

So I went to his house.

AJ, what is all this stuff? Don't you think you're taking this vampire thing too far?
It's research. I have this feeling . . . that something's not right.
With what?
We need Nia!

CHAPTER 7

Now isn't the time for girlfriends!
No, it's time for slayers.

You're sure this is her house?
This is where her birthday party was last year.
Gimme your phone. I'll text her.
I . . . I don't have her number.
Use your own phone.
Fine.
Hey, Nia. It's AJ.
From school.
I'm using Ivy's phone.
Are you awake?

Are you sure this is a good idea?
Positive.
What if she's asleep?
I don't know.
We need your help!

Forget this. I'm throwing a rock. It worked with you.
Don't!

BWEEP! BWEEP! BWEEP!
Oh, crud! My stupid search alert! Why is it so loud?!

AJ? Ivy? Is that you guys?

Guess who bought
Bran Castle?!

Oh,
I already know.

You fixed it!

I'll be right down!
Hang on.

What is all this stuff?
You're about to find out.

Let me get this straight, you think Mr. Niles is a vampire?
Bingo.
And you say Hunter's missing, right?

Yeah, but I don't know what Mr. Niles has against him.
I do.

How'd you figure it out without his phone?
Books!
Nice!

Wait, wait, wait! Pull over!

You have our teacher's phone?

Yep! Check it.
UNLOCKED!

You have his password?! How?

Well . . .

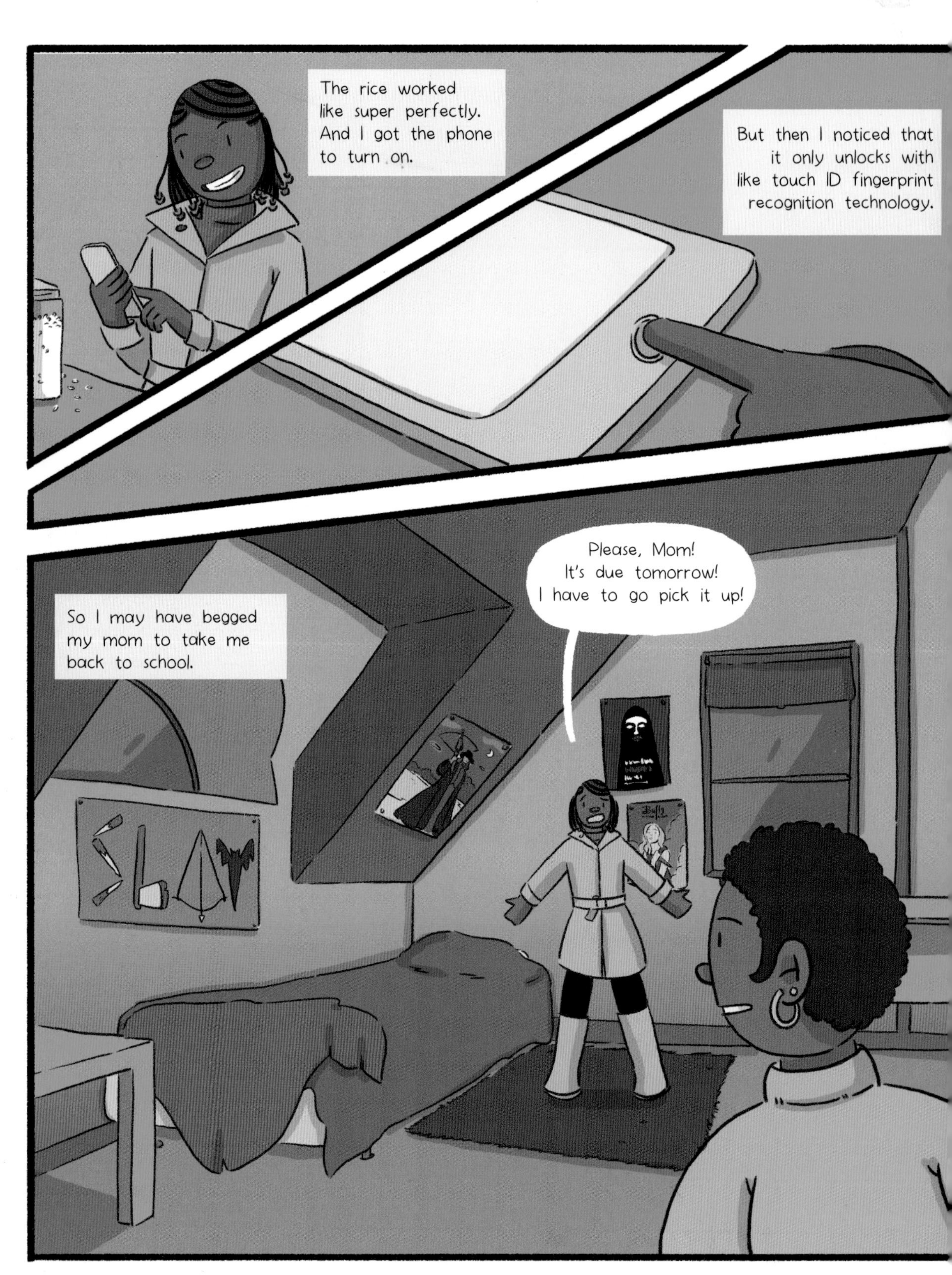
The rice worked like super perfectly. And I got the phone to turn on.
But then I noticed that it only unlocks with like touch ID fingerprint recognition technology.
So I may have begged my mom to take me back to school.
Please, Mom! It's due tomorrow! I have to go pick it up!

SPOONS MIDDLE SCHOOL
So Mom waited in the car while I did a little digging.
Then all it took was a little tape.
Bingo.

No biggie.

What are you? Some sort of CSI vampire hunter?

So then I went through his texts.
And look what I found!

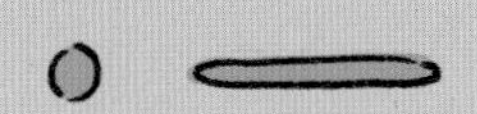

IVAN

I'm telling you! The little brute is terrifying. Totally unhinged.

And what? You're trying to tell me the Fang Agreement of 1992 is just . . . out the window? He won't attack you. It's the law.

He's too young to know about 1992. And you know young wolves, they're not the brightest.

If you're really that worried, get rid of him. Make it quiet. You'll be fine. No one has to know.

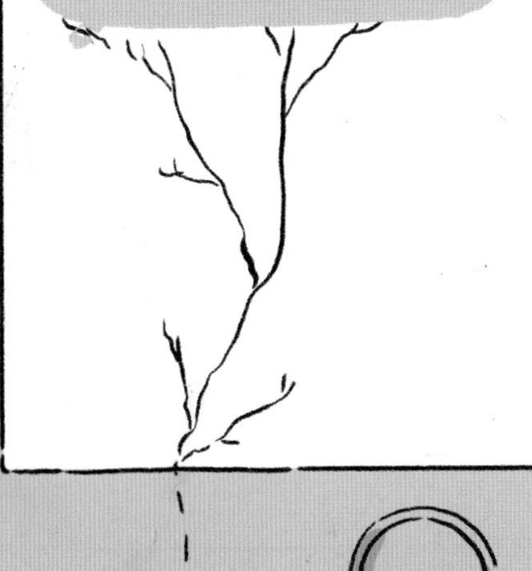

But he could be anywhere!
Nia? Any ideas?
Are there any caves nearby?

Not that I know of.

I thought you were obsessed with this stuff!

Don't be mean. Maybe it's in the phone.
I tried. Nothing but a bunch of weird apps.

SUBSCRIBE

CRUELTY-FREE BLOOD
FOR THE SOCIALLY CONSCIOUS

One is for some type of weird vegan blood delivery service.

THIS WEEK'S SELECTIONS

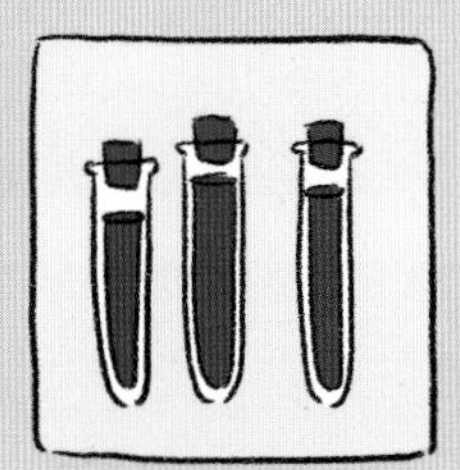

THE FIENDSTER

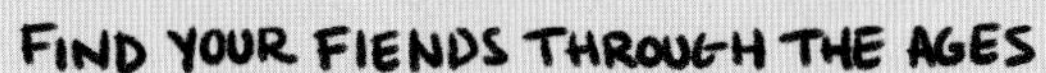

ARTEMIS ALVAH "LIVE LIKE U COULD DIE."

- THE NIGHT
- VEGAN PLZ
- IT'S COMPLICATED

And another is full of vintage-y pictures of some woman.

But nothing has his address.

Where did they hide out in *Moonlight*? Underground?

UGH! *Moonlight* isn't REAL.

Some of it might be. Up until today I thought vampires weren't real.

I looked everywhere. I couldn't find any clues.

It didn't matter that I got into his phone. I don't even know what color his house is.

Oh.
My.
GOODNESS!
I know
where he is!

Race you there!
BUMPS
AHEAD

Ta-da!
I don't get it.
Me either.

Don't you remember? Mr. Niles was all . . .
Blimey! What a jolly good shirt you have! Why it's the same cracking color as my house, by Jove!

But this isn't a house.

Maybe he meant he lives in a red house?

Are you kidding?

This has to be it.

AROOOOOOOOU
That's Hunter!
I told you!
Hey, guys?
Check this out.

AROOO
Stop your howling, beast!

I told you, it's a full moon! You'll be sorry!
GRRL
SNRL

No it isn't. It's a waning gibbous.

A waning what?

Werewolves. Always thinking you're so clever.

HOWOOOo
AWO
I said stop howling or I'll make you stop!

OOO

Get away from him!

Well, isn't this just adorable?
My bitsy baby students show up, to what?
Rescue their mangy classmate?

I'd let him go if I were you!
CRUNCH!
That isn't gonna do it.

I'm four hundred years old! And you think a little allium sativum is going to stop me?

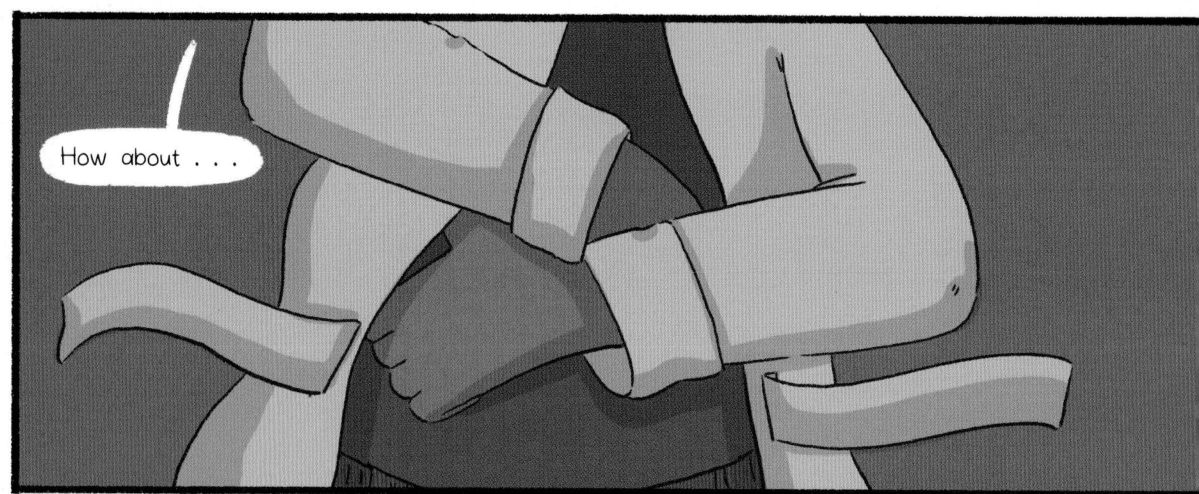
How about . . .

HOLY
H2O
this?
NARF

Okay, that might.

Go!
Save yourselves!

Jump!

Jump?!
Are you nuts?

Now, now, young lady. You don't know who you're dealing with here.
Back up!

It'll be just like this summer!
Oh yeah!

What are you talking about?

Bungee jumping!

Oh. I uh . . . I lied.
WHAT?!
I know I said I jumped, but . . . I couldn't do it. I was too scared.
I'm warning you!
And I'm warning you. Let him down.

Go climb up and get him.
Huh?

I can't climb all the way up there!

But—Mount St. Helens—you said . . .
Oh, Ivy, not you, too?!

Sorry.

It's okay.
I got this.

SQUIRT!
WOOSH!
CRASH!
AGH!
NOOOOO!

Now,
I didn't want this to get so out of hand.
I didn't want to have to involve anyone. I was more than happy to leave you out of it.

Especially you, Mr. AJ. But you've seen too much. You'll report me to the council and I can't have that.

I'm sorry. But you'll all have to perish.

How did I mess it all up so badly?

BRRING!
My mobile? You have my mobile?!
Give it here!

Artemis! I knew you'd come around!

What do you mean the last time?

You can't mean that. Not after everything—

I bought you a castle! I've signed the paperwork and everything.

You're what?! You can't be serious!

No, this is not good-bye! It can't—

All right, beast!

Your time on this earth has finally run out.

Bloody hell, hound, how much sugar do you eat?! You reek!

This is the worst day of my life.
I can't believe she isn't coming.

Who are you even talking about?

You'd never understand. You're only eleven.
Your lives are all so boring.

That's what I keep saying!

It can't be all that bad.
Oh, but it is! What am I going to do now? I'm ruined!

It looks like you got a pretty okay thing going to me.

BB! Get us out of here!

I mean, hey, you got a sweet hideout, a killer accent. What's to be so bummed out about?
Look, I'm fifteen. I know what's what.

What's got you so bummed out?

Well . . .
Oh, would you like a—

No thanks.

Ever since I turned four hundred, I noticed a change in my darling Artemis. She was always out, returning at odd hours. And she got mean.
Was she shady with her phone?
Yes! And she changed all of her passwords.

Psst.
I think I can use my pin to get us out of this.
I'm an expert lockpick.

And I just couldn't keep up with her. She's only 352 years old. So, you know she's very hip.
Sounds like it.

And I know we've all agreed to go with cruelty-free options. But this stuff is like drinking beet-flavored mucus.

Gross!

You're gross, Gummy Bear!

Now, now, there's no need for name calling. What happened next?

She left me. For a much younger man. One of those . . . hipster vamps with all the hair gel.

Well, then she wasn't the one for you anyway.
I bet he even knows how to use VampChat.

There, there. Who wants to spend eternity with a girl like that?

I did!
And I'm not finished!
Okay, okay.
I thought I would move to Portland to start over. Move on with my life. Forget her. But how could I? It's so bleak here.
Well, that's, like, your opinion.

So I devised a plan. I would invite her to move here. We could start over and keep Portland weird together or something.
Yeah, you're pretty weird, all right.

But that wouldn't be enough to impress her. Not when she's off having grand adventures with that prismatic cad.
She wants excitement, not some boring old vamp like me.

So what did I do? I went and bought her Bran Castle!
VLAD'S ACTUAL CASTLE!

Whoa.

And you know how she thanks me? She tells me she's marrying him!

Ouch.
Quite.

CRASH!

You! You were tricking me!
Yeah, a bit.
But I couldn't just let you kill my brother and all his friends.

I'll have you know one of his little *friends* is a werewolf.
And— brace yourself— your brother is a vampire!

Yeah . . . I don't think so.

What?

We kind of lied about all that.
Yeah, we were just . . . pretending.

Why would you pretend to be a vampire?

I thought it would make me . . . cool.

You think I'm cool?!

Uhh, sure.

That's the nicest thing anyone has ever said to me.

Listen, Mr. Niles, none of this is gonna make you feel any better. You could drain every last one of us, but Artemis is still gonna marry that dude.
So, go. You own a sweet castle. Live it up. Meet some vampire ladies with their own hair gel and rainbows and those cute cat-eye sunglasses yourself.

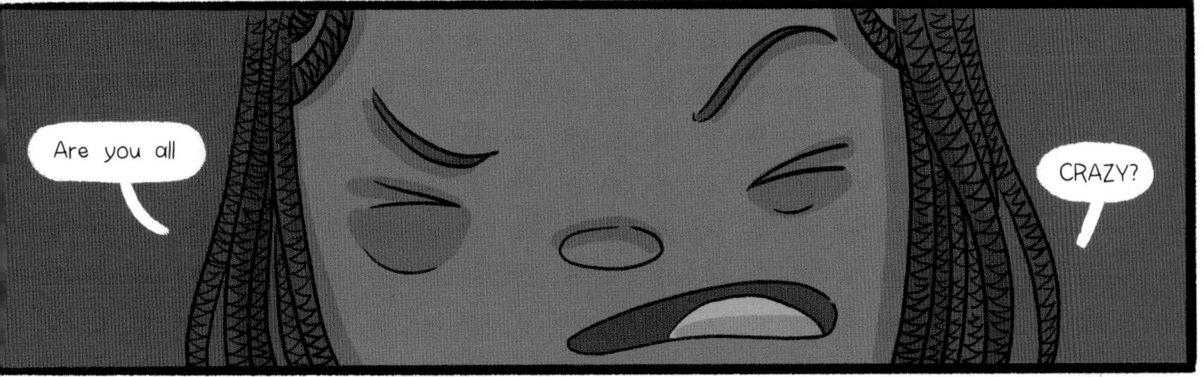
Are you all
CRAZY?

Have you lost your dang bananas?
We can't just let him go off to Bran Castle!

Why not?

Because he's a vampire!
Hello?
He threatened to kill all of us!

She has a point.
Hmm . . .

Of course I have a point!

There!

I say we take care of this once and for all!

I haven't drained a soul since 1992! I fell in line.
It certainly looked like you were ready to break your streak.

And you told me you hated the fake blood!

No, it's delicious. Really.

One day I'm sure you'll be hungry enough for the good stuff that you'll—

It won't be anyone important!

Yeah, right.

No children either. Okay?

NOT ENOUGH GOOD!
Take pity!

WAIT!
Didn't you all finish *Moonlight*?

Yeah?

Yeah?

Obviously.

Are you kidding me?

Eamon swears that he'll never drain a person again. And from then on he only hunts and drains animals.

Could he even hunt in Transylvania?

Of course! Romania is home to Europe's largest population of brown bears.
Not only brown bears, wolves, too!
You two must have worked so hard on your project!

Do you think, if it came to it, you could stick to bears and beasts?
They probably have more blood.
And better diets.
moonlight

Hunting bears? What do you take me for? A lumberman?

It's lumberjack.

Maybe start with the smaller animals? Like a raccoon?
Pathetic.
But you'll get better and better and you'll take down those grizzlies in no time.
Oh, man, a guy who could take down a bear, with his bare fangs?
That's very impressive.

You really think?
Absolutely.

Yes! Well, okay then! From here on out I shall do my very best to only—

Ahem!

Okay, okay, fine.

From this moment forward, I, Remington Niles, promise never to drain another human being as long as I shall live.
MOONLIGHT

Now, begone. I've had enough of you for two lifetimes. And I'll live forever.
You don't have to tell me twice.
Let's go, kiddos!

Have fun in Transylvania. I'm sure you'll meet someone new in no time.

Just be yourself!
But how?

Yes! I win!
Ugh, there was a breeze.

I really am sorry about trying to slay you.
I told you, it's okay. I'm sorry you didn't get to fulfill your, like, destiny.
Honestly . . . I'm kind of glad.

Really?
Yeah.
Like I don't think I'm actually ready to . . .
You know, anyone. Vampire or otherwise.
I think you're still pretty brave anyway.
And you're, like, the least boring kid I know.

You think Mr. Niles will keep his word?

He better. You still got that search alert thing?
Oh yeah!

Maybe you should keep it on.
Just in case.

Oh! I heard the new *Natalie and the Ninja Star* comes out next week.

Already?

You still want to go to Powell's with me?
Totally! I'm gonna get the first copy they put on the shelf!

Wanna bet?

HALL OF FAME

Thanks to everyone who has supported me and my goofy book.
Your wisdom, enthusiasm, and kindness has meant the world to me.

READY

FAKE BLOOD
FAKE BLOOD
FAKE BLOOD
FAKE BLOOD
FAKE BLOOD

FAKE BLOOD
FAKE BLOOD
FAKE BLOOD
FAKE BLOOD
FAKE BLOOD
FAKE BLOOD